THE BOY WHO CRIED POO!

Brimming with creative inspiration, how-to projects, and useful information to enrich your everyday life, quarto.com is a favourite destination for those pursuing their interests and passions.

Inspiring | Educating | Creating | Entertaining

The Boy Who Cried Poo © 2023 Quarto Publishing plc
Text © 2023 Alessandra Requena. Illustrations © 2023 Guilherme Karsten

First published in 2023 by Frances Lincoln Children's Books,
an imprint of The Quarto Group.
1 Triptych Place, London, SE1 9SH, United Kingdom.
T (0)20 7700 6700 F (0)20 7700 8066
www.Quarto.com

The right of Guilherme Karsten to be identified as the illustrator and
Alessandra Requena to be idendtified as the author of this work has
been asserted by them in accordance with the Copyright, Designs and
Patents Act, 1988 (United Kingdom).

A catalogue record for this book is available from the
British Library.

ISBN 978-0-7112-7946-9
eBook ISBN 978-0-7112-7949-0

The illustrations were created digitally.

Set in ArcherPro

Published and edited by Peter Marley
Designed by Zoë Tucker
Production by Dawn Cameron

Manufactured in Guangdong, China TT122022

1 3 5 7 9 8 6 4 2

MIX
Paper from
responsible sources
FSC® C016973
FSC
www.fsc.org

For Marc who can take a joke,
and for my Dad, Mauro, who
usually can't. Enjoy! – A.R.

To Lucca and Vicente, our poop
stories have become the funniest
memories – G.K.

THE BOY WHO CRIED POO!

Alessandra
Requena

Frances Lincoln
Children's Books

Guilherme
Karsten

The sun was bright and hot on the first day of our holiday. My little brother, Marc, and I couldn't wait to go down to the pool. "Everybody ready?" asked Dad.

"YES!" we said.

"Does anyone need to go to the bathroom?"

"NO!"

So we waved goodbye to Mum, Papo and Bella and promised to save them the best seats by the pool. There was a tower of stairs to get down...

exactly 168 steps.
(I'd counted.)

Down,

down,

down

we raced, excited to be the first ones to jump in.

We were the first ones in!
We jumped into the calm water with a...

SPLaSH!!

And that's when Marc said...

"DAD! I HAVE TO POO!"

"Uh-oh! Let's go!" said Dad.

So we got out, dried off
and climbed back up.

up

up,

Up,

all 168 steps. We passed three old ladies in fuzzy sweaters, two kids with rubber rings and one pregnant lady balancing a tray of bacon.

Finally, we got back to the top.
Dad threw open the door, tossed
Marc on the loo and...

"I don't have to go anymore."

"Well, good try, buddy!" said Dad,
who was looking a little sweaty.
"You'd better hurry back down or you
won't find good seats," said Mum.

So down we went.

Down,
down,
down

the tower stairs...

past a man with a
crate of 200 churros,

past a girl with
three dogs in spiky collars,
back to the pool.

We weren't the only ones there now...

Dad sat down with a sigh,
and we jumped in with a...

SPLASH!

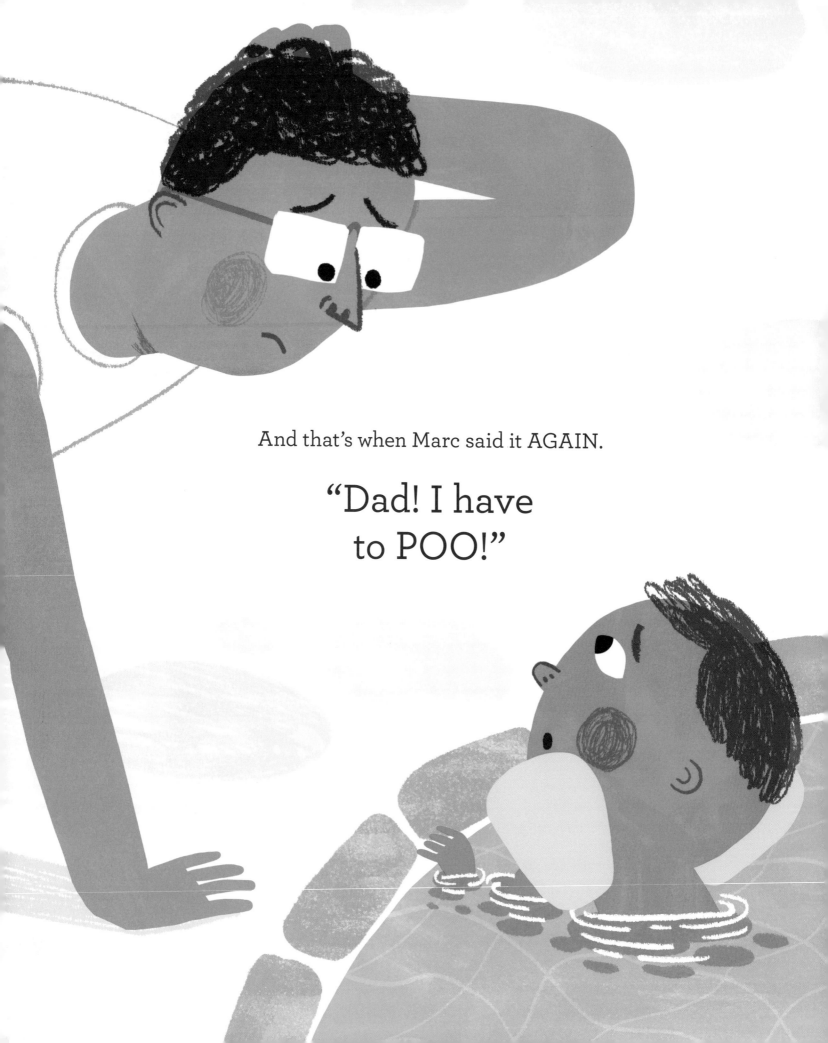

And that's when Marc said it AGAIN.

"Dad! I have to POO!"

"Are you joking? We just got in again," I said. But it was no joke.

"No, I really, really have to poo.
RIGHT NOW!"

So we climbed out, dripping all over the place, and ran back up the stairs. Because when you gotta go, you gotta go!

Marc got tired halfway up,

so Dad carried him under his arm like a football.

Up,
up,
up

past
someone
suspicious in
a pink bird
costume,

JILL?

past a crew of pirates
looking for a girl named Jill,

past thirteen angry cats.

Finally, we got back to the top.

Dad kicked open the door, hurled
Marc at the loo and...

"I don't have to go anymore."

"Try putting your feet up while you push," said Papo.

"Try drinking a glass of water while you push," said Bella.

"Just poop already!" I said.

"But I don't have to go anymore!" said Marc.

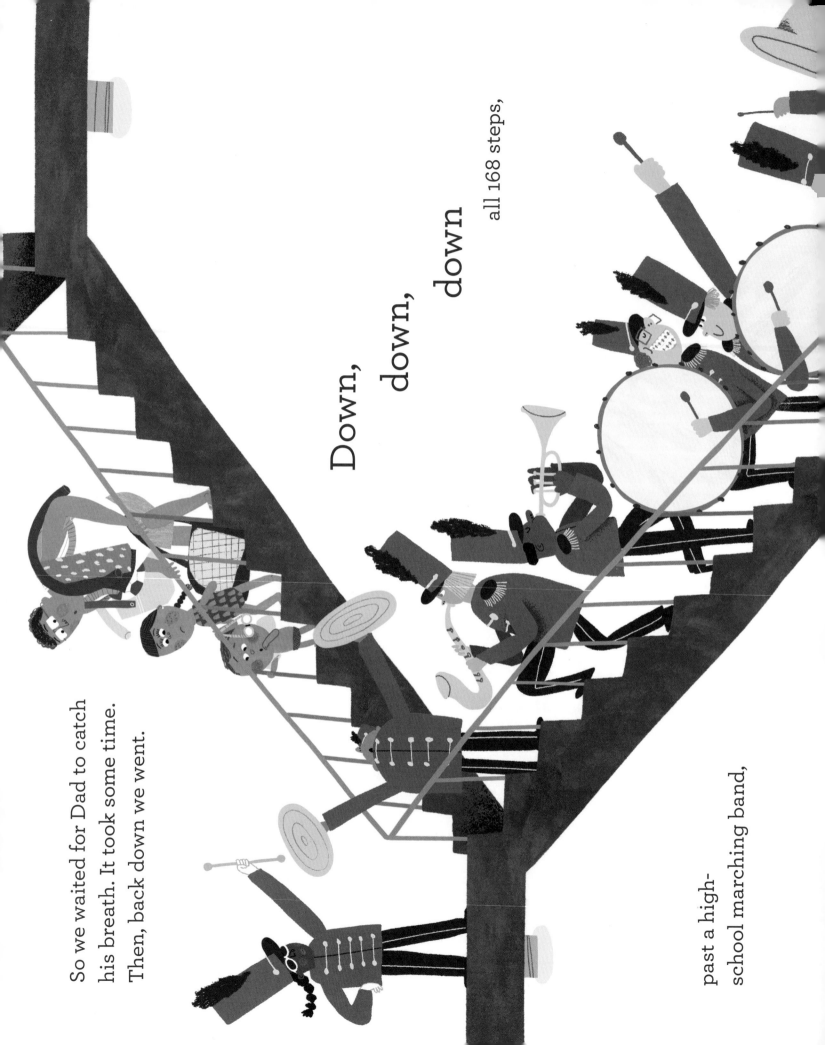

So we waited for Dad to catch his breath. It took some time. Then, back down we went.

Down,

down,

down

all 168 steps,

past a high-school marching band,

past a group of construction workers
carrying a seven-foot tall bronze statue
of Sor Juana Inés de la Cruz,

past three molting
flamingos hopping
down the stairs...

back to the pool.
We definitely weren't the only ones there now.
All the same we jumped in with a...

SPLASH!

I wish I could say that we swam happily ever after, but...

"Dad, I need to poo."

This time, Dad didn't jump up to grab him. "No, I can't... I can't go back up."

"But, Dad, I REALLY
need to poo!"

"Please, just try and hold
it in," said Dad.

"But I reaaaaalllllly
have to go!"

"Maybe it will pass.
Again," insisted Dad.

I watched Marc scrunch his
face up, and I wasn't so sure.
"Dad," I said, "I think he really
does have to go this time."

But it was too late.
It was done.

"Dad... I went poo."

Sure enough, there it was:

A SINKER

Everyone climbed out of the pool.

It was silent for a minute as they
stared at Marc.

Then one of the construction workers took off her hat. "One time, I pooped in a pool," she said.

"Arrr, I pooped on the deck once," said a pirate.

"I pooed in my good trousers, and that's why I'm wearing this costume," said the guy in the bird costume.

"I think I just pooped! Someone call the doctor, this baby is coming!" said the pregnant lady.

Soon, the marching band was playing, and everyone was sharing their accidental-poo stories.

"I pooed in my snowsuit last winter at school," I told Marc. "Dad had to come and get me." "No way!" said Marc, who was eating an ice cream someone had brought him.

By the time Mum, Papo and Bella came
down, the water was sparkly clean again.
And now whenever someone has an
accident, Marc and I tell them our stories...

because
everyone poops
their pants sometimes.

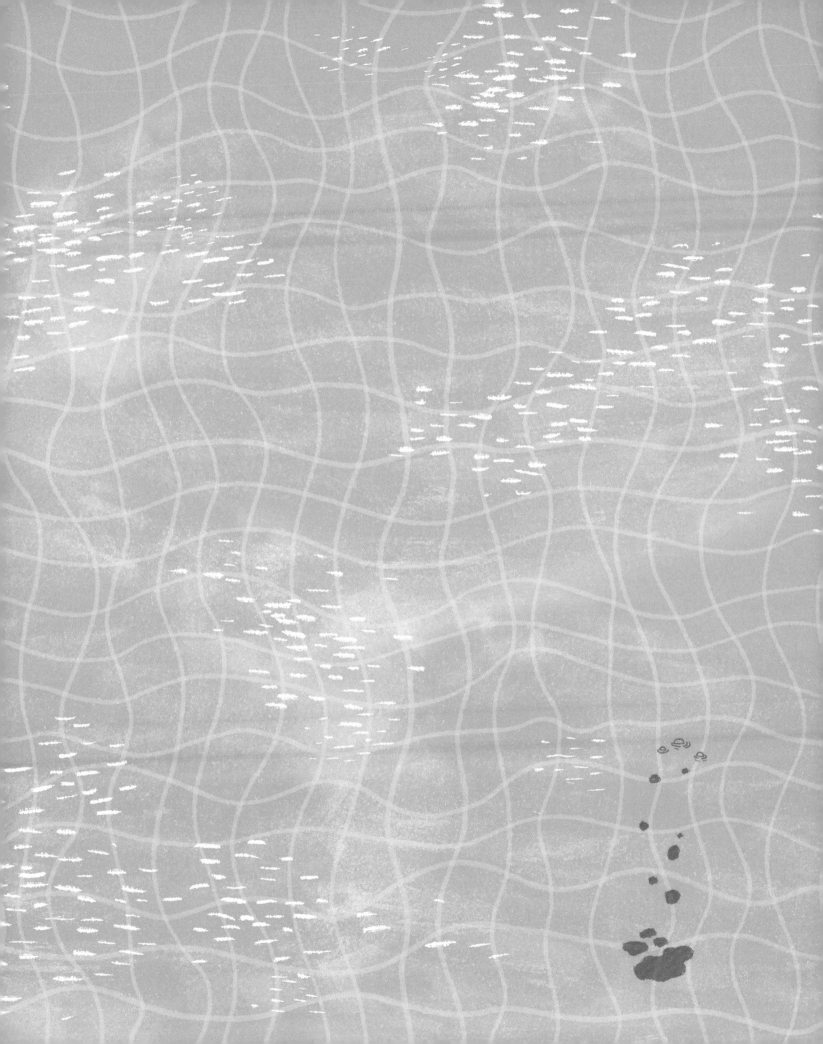